G *is for* **Goat**

To Nancy and Donna . . . *lovers of goats.*
And especially to Belle.

PATRICIA POLACCO

G is for **Goat**

PHILOMEL BOOKS

A is for Apple,
the best treat of all.

B is for Billy,
what boy goats are called.

C is for Cart
that billy pulls fast.

D is for Dog,
which we try to pass.

E is for Ears,
some floppy, some not.

F is for Flowers,
which goats eat a lot.

G is for Goats,
they nibble my nose,
billies and bucks, nannies and does.

H is for Hay,
what I feed my friend Patch.

I is for Itches,
I laugh when they scratch.

J is for Jump,
what kids do with such joy.

Kids are goat children like our girls and boys.

L is for Lunch—
get out of their way!

M is for Munch;
clothes taste better than hay.

N is for Nanny,
whose milk can't be beat.

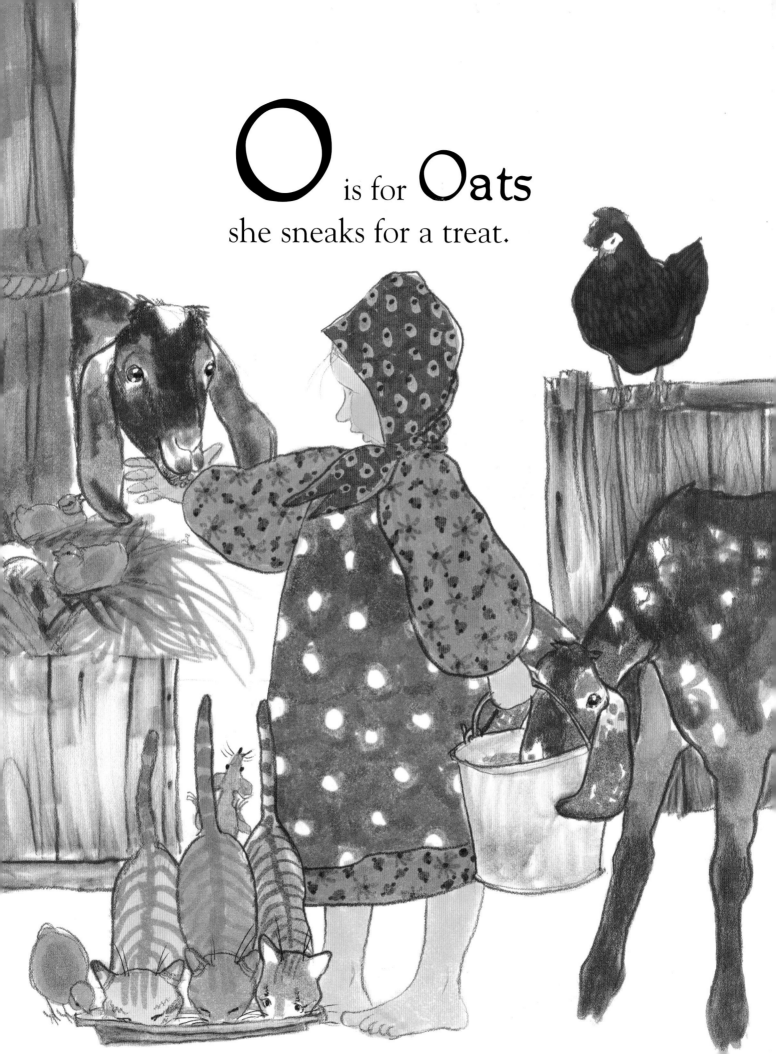

O is for Oats

she sneaks for a treat.

P is for Push,

when goats just won't go.

Q is for Quit,
when goats just say no.

R is for Ram,
when they butt heads for fun.

S is for Spots,

what they see when they're done.

T is for Tails,
they wag and they shake.

U is for Up,
what good climbers they make!

V is for Vet—
we think something's wrong!

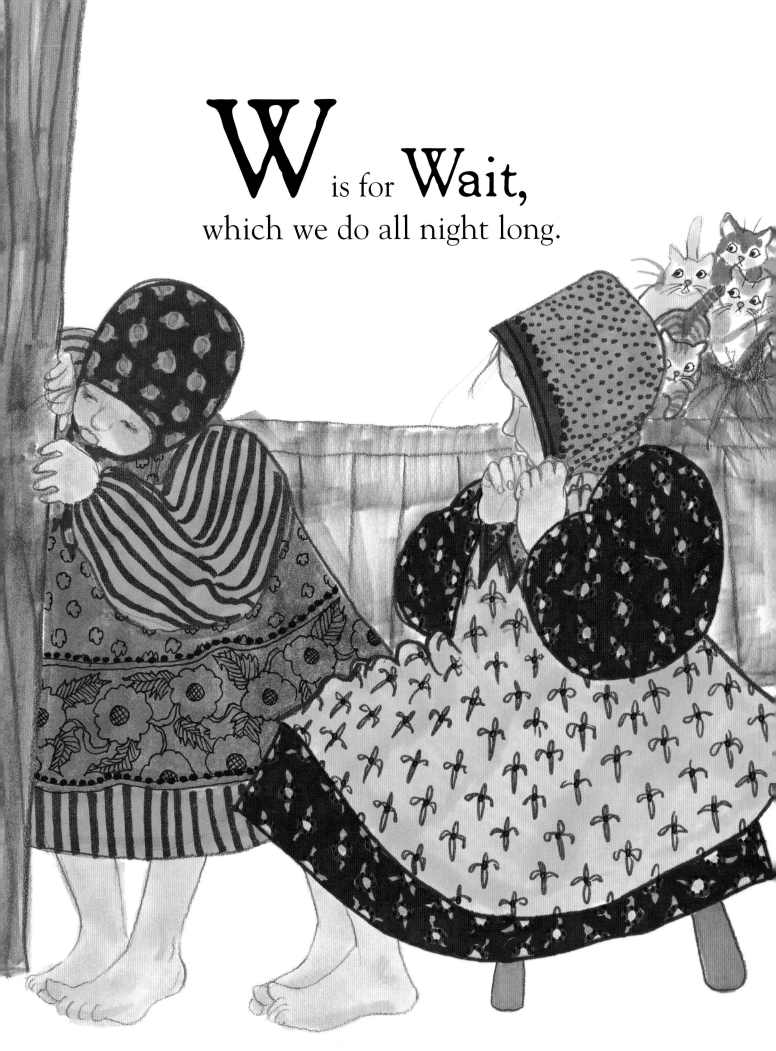

W is for Wait,
which we do all night long.

X, I'm eXcited ...
just look what's new!

Y is for sweet, adorable You!

Z . . . amaZing!
Three babies came . . .
Zig, Zag and Zoë will be their names.

Patricia Lee Gauch, editor

Book design by Semadar Megged.
The text is set 25-point Goudy.
The illustrations are rendered in pencil and watercolor.

Library of Congress Cataloging-in-Publication Data
Polacco, Patricia.
G is for goat / Patricia Polacco ; Patricia Lee Gauch, editor.
p. cm.
Summary: A rhyming celebration of goats and their antics, from A to Z.
[1. Goats—Fiction. 2. Alphabet. 3. Stories in rhyme.]
I. Gauch, Patricia Lee. II. Title. PZ8.3.P55895 Gae 2003
[E]—dc21 2002011551
ISBN 0-399-24018-7
1 2 3 4 5 6 7 8 9 10
First Impression